Monsters' Magic Formulas

怪獸的魔法書

Stanislav Marijanovic 著／繪

張憶萍　譯

Monsters'
Magic
Formulas

三民書局

On the river bank at the edge of the forest stood the oldest house in town.

It was summer, and the family that lived in the house were leaving for their holidays. They were not in the least bit worried, because they knew that all their **mischievous** house **monsters** had **sneaked** into their **luggage** to follow them along.

So off they drove, turning to look back at their house one last time. Everything was in order, and all looked **calm**.

mischievous [ˋmɪstʃɪvəs] 形 愛惡作劇的；淘氣的
monster [ˋmɑnstɚ] 名 怪獸
sneak [snik] 動 偷偷地進出

luggage [ˋlʌgɪdʒ] 名 行李
calm [kɑm] 形 平靜的

But...Not ALL the house monsters had gone. Tickle and Pickle the **twins** had stayed behind. Tickle and Pickle were two young monsters with prickly tails. They were indoor monsters, the kind that never leave the house.

Tickle and Pickle were happy. They had the entire place to themselves. They could run and dance and climb and jump, and they could play any game they liked. "Let's play **hide-and-seek**" they decided, and they ran off to find hiding places.

Tickle was looking for a place to hide when he found himself in the darkest corner of the **cellar**. He had never been there before. As his eyes **got used to** the dark, he **discovered** an old chest held shut by a big **rusted** lock. Tickle forgot all about hide-and-seek...

twin [twɪn] 名 雙胞胎中的一個
hide-and-seek [ˌhaɪdṇˋsik] 名 捉迷藏
cellar [ˋsɛlɚ] 名 地下貯藏室

get used to... 習慣於…
discover [dɪˋskʌvɚ] 動 發現
rust [rʌst] 動 生銹

...and **set about** opening the lock. He **managed** to get the lock off quite easily, but inside the chest there was a smaller chest with two locks! Now he was really curious.

What could this chest be hiding?

Pickle arrived and started to help, **fetching** all the tools that he could find. The twins quickly opened the second chest, but they were **astonished** to discover a third chest inside with three locks!

Trembling with excitement, Tickle and Pickle continued their work. Inside the third chest there was a fourth, and inside the fourth was a fifth and then a sixth chest which at last **revealed** the secret.

"It's an old book!" cried Pickle from inside the chest. The twins decided to take it upstairs to see what it was about.

set about... 開始做…
manage [ˋmænɪdʒ] 動 設法
fetch [fɛtʃ] 動 拿來

astonish [əˋstɑnɪʃ] 動 使吃驚
reveal [rɪˋvil] 動 洩露

But the book was much too heavy for them to carry, so Pickle fetched some wheels and pulleys and they **hoisted** the book to the top of the stairs.

It was an old book **bound** in leather and silver. "It's written in Monster Language!" cried Tickle, and the twins set about **deciphering** the title. It wasn't easy at all. There were letters that the little monsters had never seen before, but they managed to **figure out** the title nonetheless:

"The Book of Magic **Formulas**"

How to **transform** things...

        Instructions for **turning** one thing **into** another...

              Formulas, lots of formulas, one after another...

hoist [hɔɪst] 動 吊起
bind [baɪnd] 動 裝訂
decipher [dɪˋsaɪfɚ] 動 辨認；解讀
figure out 了解

formula [ˋfɔrmjələ] 名 法則
transform [trænsˋfɔrm] 動 轉換；變化
instruction [ɪnˋstrʌkʃən] 名 指示；命令
turn...into... 將⋯變成⋯

The little monsters looked at each other: "Let's try the formulas," they decided without a second thought.

Pickle quickly **browsed** through the book and **stuttered** the first short formula he **ran across**. Of course Pickle could not read all that well, and his brother Tickle didn't turn into a toad as Pickle **intended**.

But he did turn...

browse [brauz] 動 隨意翻閱 《through》　　　intend [ɪnˈtɛnd] 動 打算
stutter [ˈstʌtɚ] 動 結結巴巴地說
run across 偶然發現

...into a funny WINGED-TOAD-LIKE-THING.

Pickle laughed so loud that he didn't realize that the WINGED-TOAD-LIKE-THING had taken the book and was looking for another formula.

Soon Pickle stopped laughing, because he found himself transformed into a TWO-HEADED-CARROTOID.

It was now Tickle's **turn** to laugh,
but the TWO-HEADED-CARROTOID
quickly transformed him into a
FLUFFY SPIDER-HEN.

turn [tɜn] 图 順序

The mischief continued with unstoppable **hysterical** laughter as the book was passed from Tickle to Pickle and back again. **Needless to say**, not one magic formula was pronounced correctly!

Throughout the afternoon, through the windows of the oldest house in town, the strangest creatures could be seen **appearing** and **disappearing**:

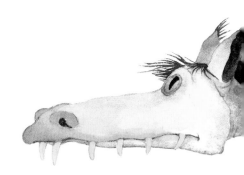

the MANGO-WINGED-PARROTMOUSE

hysterical [hɪsˈtɛrɪkl] 形 歇斯底里般的
needless to say 不用說；當然
appear [əˈpɪr] 動 出現

disappear [ˌdɪsəˈpɪr] 動 消失

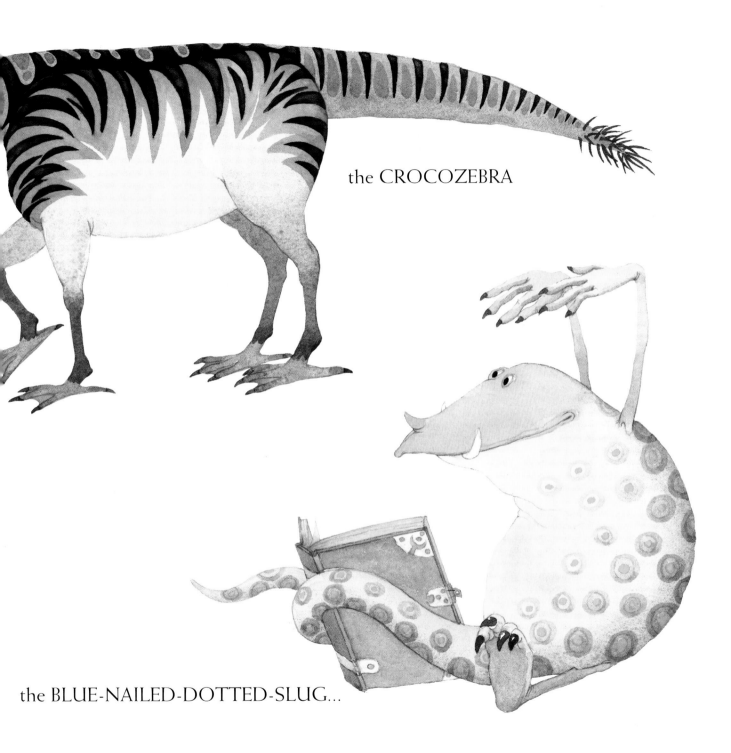

the CROCOZEBRA

the BLUE-NAILED-DOTTED-SLUG...

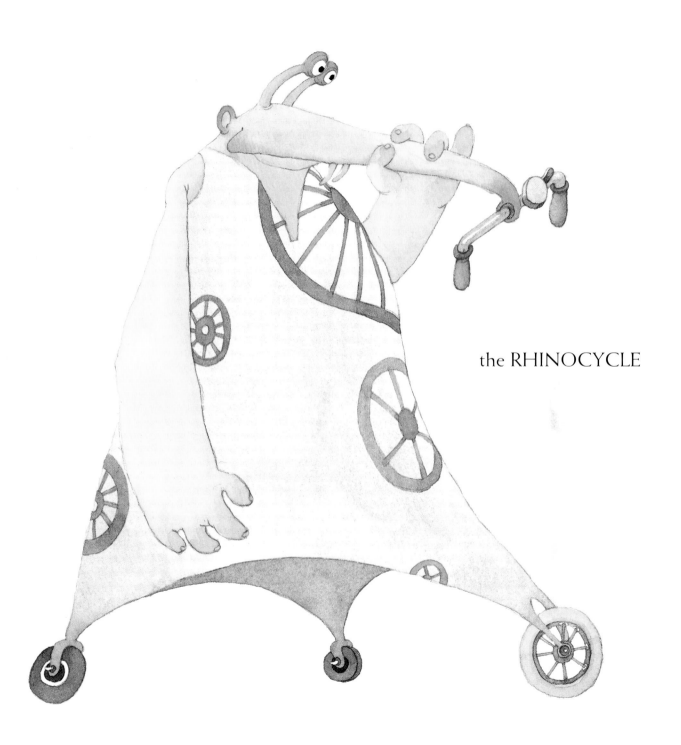

the RHINOCYCLE

the DANCING-DRAINPIPE…

the SIX-EYED-EGG (with tail)

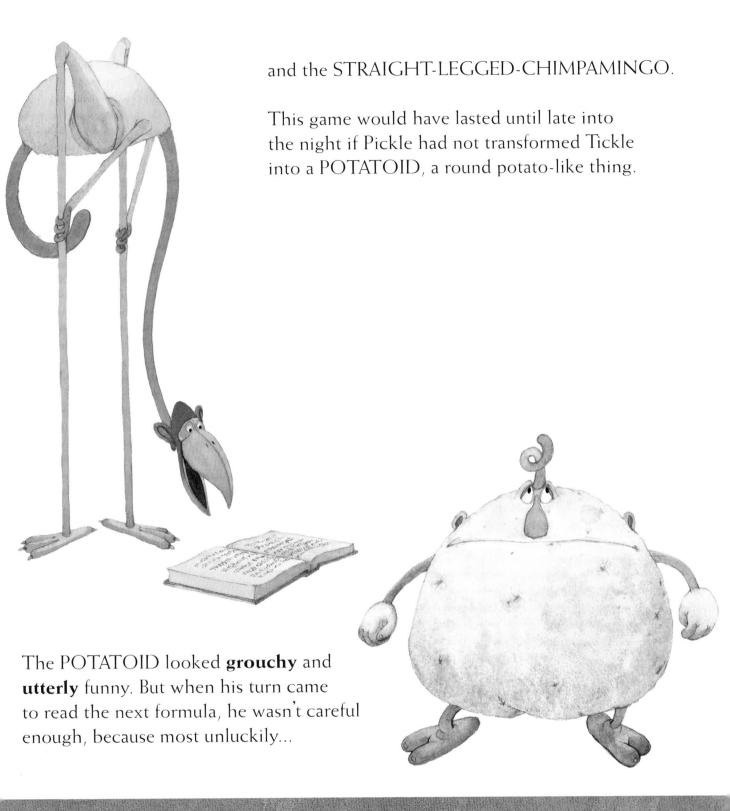

and the STRAIGHT-LEGGED-CHIMPAMINGO.

This game would have lasted until late into the night if Pickle had not transformed Tickle into a POTATOID, a round potato-like thing.

The POTATOID looked **grouchy** and **utterly** funny. But when his turn came to read the next formula, he wasn't careful enough, because most unluckily...

grouchy [ˋɡraʊtʃɪ] 形 脾氣壞的
utterly [ˋʌtɚlɪ] 副 完全地

...THE POTATOID transformed his twin brother into a **fierce** STRIPED-POTATO-EATER.

The STRIPED-POTATO-EATER looked at the POTATOID and started **drooling**. Without thinking twice, he jumped to catch him and eat him, forgetting entirely that it was his own brother.

"It's me, don't you see?" the POTATOID cried **desperately**, but **to no avail**. The POTATOID threw the Book of Magic Formulas behind him and he started running for his life. He paid little attention to the pages that flew out and **scattered** on the kitchen floor.

fierce [fɪrs] 形 殘暴的
drool [drul] 動 流口水
desperately [ˈdɛsprətlɪ] 副 絕望地

avail [əˈvel] 名 效用（=use）
to no avail 不起作用
scatter [ˈskætɚ] 動 散落

Nothing in the house was **spared**. Furniture, pots and lamps flew through the air and **crashed** to the floor.

spare [spɛr] 動 赦免
crash [kræʃ] 動 發出巨響摔落

Trying to find a safe place to hide, the POTATOID jumped into a large pot and pulled the lid over his head without thinking of what would happen next. "That's perfect!" cried the **greedy** STRIPED-POTATO-EATER.

But just **at that moment**, when the STRIPED-POTATO-EATER thought he had the POTATOID **trapped**...

greedy [ˋgridɪ] 形 貪婪的
at that moment 在那時
trap [træp] 動 使中計

...the front door **burst** open with a bang, and there stood Gordobax the Terrible, the **notorious** big bad monster who lived in the nearby forest.

A long time ago Gordobax lived with humans the way most monsters do. But, alas, humans were not as evil as he would have liked. So he had moved to the forest where he planned his **mischief** alone. He spent the day hiding in **abandoned** animal caves, and spent the night **lurking** around the town, looking for trouble.

Gordobax **despised** humans, and he despised all House Monsters as well, even though they were his distant **relatives**.

But what did Gordobax the Terrible want that night and why was he standing at the front door?

burst [bɝst] 動 突然發生
notorious [noˋtorɪəs] 形 惡名昭彰的
mischief [ˋmɪstʃɪf] 名 惡作劇
abandon [əˋbændən] 動 拋棄

lurk [lɝk] 動 鬼鬼祟祟地行動
despise [dɪˋspaɪz] 動 鄙視
relative [ˋrɛlətɪv] 名 親戚

"Good thing I was **passing by**," said Gordobax, "I saw the **tricks** you were **up to** through the window."

pass by 經過
trick [trɪk] 名 惡作劇
up to 做;從事

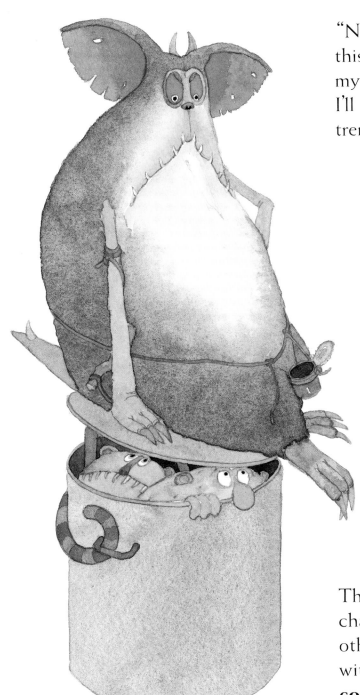

"Now," he added **gruffly**, "I will take this book for myself. I need it for my own mischief. With this book I'll make the forest and the town tremble before me with fear."

The twins forgot all about their chase and **squeezed** against each other in the cooking pot, **quaking** with fear. You could hear the **constant** clackety-clack of the lid.

gruffly [ˈgrʌflɪ] 副 粗暴地
squeeze [skwiz] 動 壓擠
quake [kwek] 動 震動

constant [ˈkɑnstənt] 形 連續不斷的

27

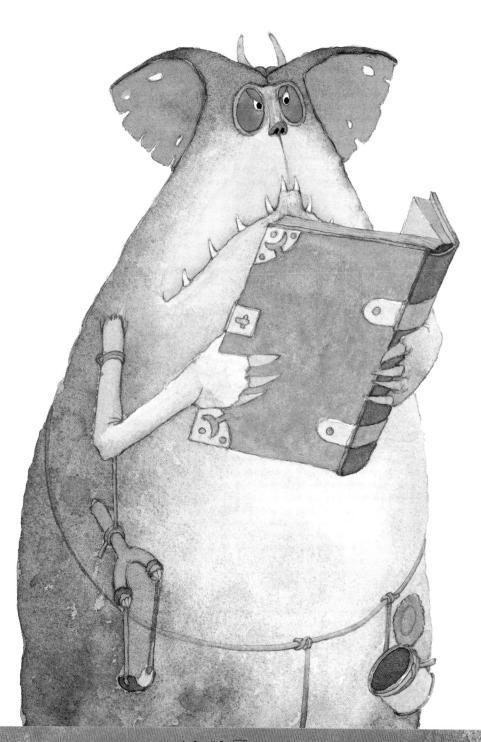

Gordobax took the book and **tucked** it under his arm. He **was about to** leave when a most wicked idea **occurred** to him.

"Before I go, I have a nice little surprise for you," said Gordobax. "I don't care what you were before, but now I will transform you into... into ..." Gordobax **paused** a little before deciding...

"That's it! I will transform you into two **hideous**, unimportant little indoor monsters with prickly tails!"

tuck [tʌk] 勔 把…塞入…
be about to... 正要做…
occur [əˋkɝ] 勔 想起 《to》

pause [pɔz] 勔 暫停
hideous [ˋhɪdɪəs] 形 醜惡的

28

The pot lid stopped **rattling at once**, and as Gordobax read the right formula, two little indoor monsters - Tickle and Pickle - **popped** out from the pot...

rattle [`ræt!] 勔 發出嘎嘎聲
at once 立刻
pop [pɑp] 勔 突然行動

...and **vanished** into the first safe place they could find: Tickle **slid** under the cooker and Pickle jumped into a drawer.

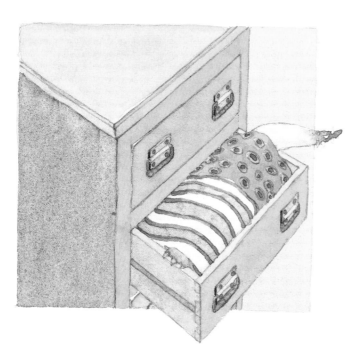

Most satisfied, Gordobax clacked the book close and **marched** off into the night.

vanish [ˋvænɪʃ] 動 消失
slide [slaɪd] 動 滑
march [mɑrtʃ] 動 大步走

Pickle **bounced** with joy, but Tickle's face was serious. He suddenly **remembered** the pages that were scattered on the kitchen floor....They were under the cooker! He had seen them while he was hiding.

"What will happen when Gordobax finds out there are pages missing from the book? **What if** he comes back to look for them?"

bounce [baʊns] 動 跳起
remember [rɪˋmɛmbɚ] 動 想起
What if...? 如果…將會怎麼樣？

Pickle **rushed** to get the pages
and as he brought them to his
brother he noticed a message
(written with big, easy-to-read
letters):

"How to make anything **invisible**".
And further on:
"If you want to make anything or
anyone invisible, you must first
say the words *swali wali dali*, then
put your finger on the red dot
and cluck three times like a
chicken."

"But **beware**:
This formula is **irreversible**."

rush [rʌʃ] 動 猛衝
invisible [ɪnˈvɪzəbl̩] 形 看不見的
beware [bɪˈwɛr] 動 當心

irreversible [ˌɪrɪˈvɚˈsəbl̩] 形 不能撤回的

The twins **exchanged** a **glance**, and smiled that **unique** mischievous smile that only house monsters can.

"Let's make the book invisible," they decided. Without wasting any time, Pickle brought the light closer and Tickle **repeated** (for the first time without any mistakes) the magic formula: *swali wali dali*, then pressed his finger against the red dot, and clucked three times like a chicken. The pages of the book vanished without a **trace**.

exchange [ɪksˋtʃendʒ] 動 交換
glance [glæns] 名 一眼
unique [juˋnik] 形 特有的

repeat [rɪˋpit] 動 複述
trace [tres] 名 蹤跡

The entire Book of Magic Formulas
also vanished from Gordobax' hands,
just as he was crossing the bridge.
He **looked around** in **amazement**,
he could not believe his eyes. "
It must have fallen into the river,"
he thought **hastily**.

ook around 四處查看
amazement [ə`mezmənt] 名 驚奇
hastily [`hestɪlɪ] 副 急速地

He **hesitated** a bit, but there was only one thing to do.
Gordobax closed his eyes, **pinched** his nose, and jumped into the water.
SPLASH!

hesitate [ˋhɛzəˌtet] 勳 猶豫
pinch [pɪntʃ] 勳 捏
splash [splæʃ] 副 噗通一聲

SPLASH! The twins heard it as they stood at the door of the house and guessed **immediately** what had happened. "Bravo" said Tickle. "He did need a bath!" and the twins **burst out** laughing.

As the stars **shone** in the sky that night, Tickle and Pickle went quietly to their beds. They didn't even **bother** to have their usual pillow-fight. There had been enough mischief for one day. Little indoor monsters never know what's **in store** for them the next day, and so they always need a good night's sleep.

 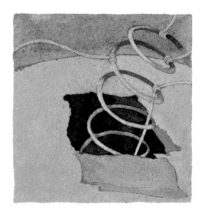

shine [ʃaɪn] 動 閃耀
bother [ˋbɑðɚ] 動 特意做
in store 即將發生 《for》

怪獸的魔法書

在森林邊緣，沿著河岸的地方，矗立著一棟全鎮最古老的房子。

現在是夏天，住在房子裡的這一家人正準備要去渡假。他們一點也不煩惱，因為他們知道家裡所有的淘氣怪獸都已經偷偷地鑽進行李箱，打算和他們一起去渡假。

他們回頭看了房子最後一眼之後，就開車上路了。一切都安排妥當，看起來也很平靜。

可是……並不是所有的怪獸都跟去了。奇奇和皮皮這一對雙胞胎可是留了下來。奇奇和皮皮是兩隻尾巴有刺的小怪獸，他們是那種從不踏出房子一步的室內怪獸。

奇奇和皮皮好高興，因為整棟房子都是他們的了。他們可以盡情跑步、跳舞、到處爬、到處跳，也可以玩任何想玩的遊戲。最後他們決定：「咱們來玩捉迷藏吧！」然後他們就開始找各自躲藏的地方。

為了找地方躲，奇奇來到地窖裡最陰暗的角落，他以前從沒來過這個地方。等到他的眼睛適應了黑暗之後，他看到一個老舊、被生銹大鎖鎖住的箱子。奇奇忘記捉迷藏這回事了……

他開始開鎖，鎖很容易就被打開了，可是在這個箱子裡，還有一個更小的箱子，上面有兩個鎖。他不禁開始感到好奇……

箱子裡裝了什麼啊？

這時皮皮也來幫忙，他拿來了所有能找到的工具，這一對雙胞胎很快的打開了第二個箱子，但令人驚訝的是，裡面放了第三個箱子，被三個鎖鎖著。

奇奇和皮皮繼續他們的工作，兩人都因為興奮而稍稍地發抖。在第三個箱子裡有第四個箱子，第四個箱子裡有第五個箱子，第五個箱子裡有第六個箱子，打開第六個箱子時，秘密終於揭曉了。

「是一本舊書！」皮皮從箱子裡大叫。他們決定把書帶到樓上，看看裡面寫了什麼。

但是書太重了，他們搬不動，於是皮皮找來了輪子和滑輪，利用它們把書吊到樓上。

這本舊書是用皮面和銀材裝訂而成的。奇奇大叫說：「它是用怪獸語言寫的！」於是這一對雙胞胎便開始解讀書名，但這工作一點也不簡單，因為有幾個字母是小怪獸從來沒見過的，不過他們還是設法猜出了書名。

「魔法書」

如何讓東西產生變化……

把一樣東西變成另一樣東西……

咒語，一大堆的咒語，一個接著一個……

這兩隻小怪獸看著對方，他們毫不猶豫的下了決定：「咱們來試試這些咒語吧！」

　　皮皮快速地將書瀏覽了一遍，然後結結巴巴地唸出他看到的第一條短咒語。當然囉，皮皮沒辦法唸得很好，所以他的哥哥奇奇也沒有如他所願地變成一隻蟾蜍。

　　不過他還是變了……

　　……變成一隻很滑稽，帶有翅膀，但長得像蟾蜍的東西。

　　皮皮笑得好大聲，完全沒有發現到這隻有翅膀，長得像蟾蜍的東西已經把書拿走，開始找尋另一條咒語了。

　　很快地皮皮停止了大笑，因為他發現自己變成了雙頭紅蘿蔔怪獸。

　　現在換奇奇大笑了，不過雙頭紅蘿蔔怪獸很快地把他變成了一隻毛絨絨的蜘蛛母雞。

　　這場惡作劇隨著此起彼落的歇斯底里笑聲持續進行，這本魔法書也在奇奇和皮皮之間傳來傳去。不用說啦，沒有一條魔咒是唸得正確的。

　　整個下午，透過鎮上最古老的房子的窗戶，可以看到最奇怪的生物出現，然後又消失。

翅膀像芒果葉的鸚鵡老鼠
鱷魚斑馬
藍指甲的圓點蛞蝓……
犀牛自行車
跳舞的排水管……
六眼蛋（有尾巴的）
還有直腳的猩猩鶴
要不是皮皮把奇奇變成一個

圓圓的、長得像洋芋的東西，這個遊戲本來可以持續到深夜的。

　　洋芋怪獸看起來不太高興，而且十分的滑稽，不過換他唸咒語的時候，他太不小心了，因為很不幸地……

　　……洋芋怪獸把自己的雙胞胎弟弟變成了一隻殘暴的斑紋食洋芋怪獸。

　　斑紋食洋芋怪獸看著洋芋怪獸，口水開始流了下來，毫不猶豫地，他撲向洋芋怪獸，打算吃了他，完全沒想到洋芋怪獸是自己的親兄弟。

　　「是我啊，你看不出來嗎？」洋芋怪獸絕望地哭叫著，可惜沒有什麼用。洋芋怪獸把魔法書丟開，開始逃命。他沒有注意到有幾頁掉了出來，散落在廚房的地板上。

　　房子裡沒有一樣東西能倖免於難。家具、鍋子、燈具，全被拋到空中，然後摔落在地上。

　　為了要找個安全的地方躲避，洋芋怪獸跳進了一個大鍋子，並把蓋子蓋上，一點也沒想到會有什麼後果。「太棒了！」貪吃的斑紋食洋芋怪獸大叫。

　　就在斑紋食洋芋怪獸覺得洋芋怪獸已經到手的時候……

　　……前門砰的一聲被撞開，站在門口的是可怕的哥德白，他是惡名昭彰的大壞獸，住在附近的森林裡。

　　很久以前，哥德白和大部份的怪獸一樣與人類同住，但是，哎呀，他覺得人類不夠壞，所以他就搬到森林裡，
在那兒獨自計劃著他的惡行。
白天，他躲在廢棄的動物巢穴，
夜裡，他就潛伏在鎮上，找
機會製造麻煩。

　　哥德白鄙視人類，

也鄙視所有的室內怪獸，即使他們是他的遠親也不例外。

但是，可怕的哥德白今天晚上要做什麼？他為何站在那兒呢？

「我正打這兒經過，」哥德白說，「我在窗外看到你們的把戲了。」

「現在，」他粗野地繼續說道，「我要把這本書帶走，用它來進行我自己的惡作劇。有了這本書，整座森林和鎮上全部的人就會在我面前害怕顫抖了。」

這對雙胞胎忘了兩人原先的追逐，現在擠在鍋子裡，害怕地發抖。你可以聽到鍋蓋一直發出喀啦喀啦的聲音。

哥德白拿起書，把它塞到腋下。就在他要離開的時候，他想到了一個最邪惡的主意。

哥德白說，「我走之前，要給你們一個小小的驚喜，我不管你們以前是什麼樣子，現在，我要把你們變成……變成……」哥德白在決定之前頓了一會兒……

「對了！我要把你們變成兩隻討人厭、不被人重視、尾巴又有刺的小型室內怪獸！」

鍋蓋立刻停止了震動，而且就在哥德白唸出正確的咒語之後，兩隻小小的室內怪獸——奇奇和皮皮——從鍋子裡跳了出來……

……然後消失在他們找到的第一個安全的地方——奇奇滑進爐灶底下，皮皮則跳進抽屜裡。

幸好，哥德白後來只是啪的一聲把書闔上，然後就邁步離開，消失在夜色中了。

　　皮皮高興得跳了起來，但奇奇卻一副嚴肅的樣子。他突然記起散落在廚房地板上的那幾張紙……在爐灶底下！他躲在那裡的時候看到的。

　　「要是哥德白發現書缺了幾頁怎麼辦？萬一他回來找怎麼辦？」

　　皮皮衝去撿那幾張紙。當他拿給哥哥奇奇的時候，他注意到上面有一段文字（用又大又容易讀的字寫成的）：

　　「如何讓東西消失」緊接著：

　　「如果你想讓某樣東西或某個人消失，你得先說『史瓦利瓦利達利』，然後把手指放在這個紅點上，再學雞一樣咯咯咯叫三聲。」

　　「但是記住：這條咒語是不能取消的。」

　　這對雙胞胎彼此對看了一眼，露出室內怪獸特有的頑皮笑容。

　　他們決定：「咱們來把書變不見好了。」皮皮馬上把燈拉近，奇奇則（第一次毫無錯誤地）唸咒語：「史瓦利瓦利達利」，接著他將手指放在紅點上，學雞叫了三聲。從魔法書掉落下來的幾頁紙一瞬間就消失得無影無蹤。

　　整本魔法書也在哥德白過橋時從他的手中消失，他驚訝的看看四周，不敢相信自己的眼睛。他很快地想到：「一定是掉到河裡了。」

　　他遲疑了一會兒，可是沒有其他的辦法可想。哥德白只好閉上眼睛，捏著鼻子，噗通一聲跳進河裡。

　　噗通！雙胞胎站在門口聽到傳來的水聲，馬上就猜到發生了什麼事。「太棒了！」奇奇說，「他的確需要洗個澡！」然後兩兄弟就大笑起來。

這一晚，當星星在天空中閃耀時，奇奇和皮皮安靜地上床睡覺。他們甚至沒有玩常玩的枕頭戰，因為這一天已經做了太多惡作劇了。小室內怪獸永遠不知道第二天會有什麼事情等著他們，所以他們晚上總是需要睡個好覺。

伍史利的大日記 I、II

─── 哈洛森林的妙生活

Linda Hayward 著／三民書局編輯部 譯

有一天，一隻叫做伍史利的大熊來到一個叫做「哈洛小森林」的地方，並決定要為這森林寫一本書，這就是《伍史利的大日記》！日記裡的每一天都有一段歷險記或溫馨有趣的小故事，不管你從哪天開始讀，保證都會有意想不到的驚喜哦！

第一本專為華人青少年編寫 以華人生活為主題的英文課外讀物

黛安的日記 ①

黃啟哲(Ronald Brown) 著／呂亨英 譯

如果你認為上英文課已經很苦了，想想看，要是你突然發現要搬到美國，並且必須跟美國小孩一起上學的話，會是什麼情況呢？這事就發生在黛安身上。想知道一個完全不會英文的中國小女孩在美國怎麼生存的嗎？看黛安的日記吧！

~ 看的繪本＋聽的繪本　童話小天地最能捉住孩子的心 ～

為孩子寫～彩色的夢

國家圖書館出版品預行編目資料

怪獸的魔法書 =The book of magic formulas /
Stanislav Marijanovic著 / 繪;張憶萍譯－－初版一
刷. －－臺北市；三民，民90
　　面； 公分－－(探索英文叢書)
中英對照
ISBN 957-14-3342-x(平裝)
1.英國語言－讀本

805.18　　　　　　　　　　　89018048

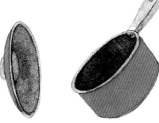

網路書店位址　http://www.sanmin.com.tw

© 怪獸的魔法書

著作兼　Stanislav Marijanovic
繪圖者
譯　者　張憶萍
發行人　劉振強
著作財　三民書局股份有限公司
產權人　臺北市復興北路三八六號
發行所　三民書局股份有限公司
　　　　地址 / 臺北市復興北路三八六號
　　　　電話 / 二五○○六六○○
　　　　郵撥 / ○○○九九九八——五號
印刷所　三民書局股份有限公司
門市部　復北店 / 臺北市復興北路三八六號
　　　　重南店 / 臺北市重慶南路一段六十一號
初版一刷　中華民國九十年一月
編　號　S 85510
定　價　新臺幣貳佰貳拾元整
行政院新聞局登記證局版臺業字第○二○○號

有著作權·不准侵害

ISBN　957-14-3342-X　 (平裝)

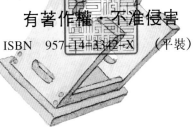